Copyright © 1991 Maureen Galvani
First published 1991 by Blackie and Son Ltd

A CIP catalogue record for this book is available from
the British Library
ISBN 0 216 93077 4

Blackie and Son Ltd
7 Leicester Place
London WC2H 7BP

Printed in Hong Kong by Wing King Tong Co. Ltd.

Me
and My Holidays

Maureen Galvani

Blackie

I get up very early to pack my things.

At last, we're here, I can see the sea.

Dad needs my help to put up the tent.

I know which jobs belong to me.

I've made a friend, she helps me build castles.

We bury Dad in a mountain of sand.

We run from the waves which tickle our toes,

and eat cold ice-cream that tickles our tums.

Dad teaches me to play cricket, I think it's great,

though sometimes Mum has a word to say.

There's a bouncing castle in the park.

I can't stand up, it wobbles so.

We look at the fishing boats way out at sea.

When they return, we buy fish for our supper.

I peep outside the tent to scare tigers and bears,

and make strange shadows with my hands.

When we go to the fair, I ride the merry-go-round,

and helter skelter down to the ground.

The ghost train is full of monsters and ghouls.

Mum and Dad need a rest to recover.

I laugh at my reflection, sometimes small, sometimes tall,

Mum gasps 'Can that really be me?'

I've packed all my things, and said my goodbyes.

At home, I show Smudge all my treasures.